Published by New Foundation Press, Inc. and
Early Beginnings Press, Pte. Ltd.

For purchases of additional copies on the internet, go to
www.newfoundationpress.com or
www.roomfordessert.net

For information about special discounts for bulk purchases,
www.newfoundationpress.com or fax 509.783.5237

We can bring authors to your live event. For more information, contact
www.newfoundationpress.com or fax to 509.783.5237.

Manufactured in China 0612 SCP
First Edition
10 9 8 7 6 5 4 3 2 1
Library of Congress Cataloging-in-Publication Data
Fielding, Lynn, 1948-
Why there is always room for dessert / Lynn Fielding –1st ed.
p. cm.
Summary: Two young children at dinner are too full to finish
their vegetables but insist that they still have room for dessert.
Their parents provide a brilliant and logical answer to this
question asked by every child.
ISBN 978-0-9666875-4-5 (hardcover)
[2013916754]

Why There Is Always

ROOM FOR DESSERT

Written by Lynn Fielding
Illustrated by Jeff Lee Johnson
Storyboard by Sonnet Fielding

Published by New Foundation Press, Inc.
and Early Beginnings Press, Pte, Ltd.

not until you finish your vegetables.

Mom, our tummies are so full
they will just pop!

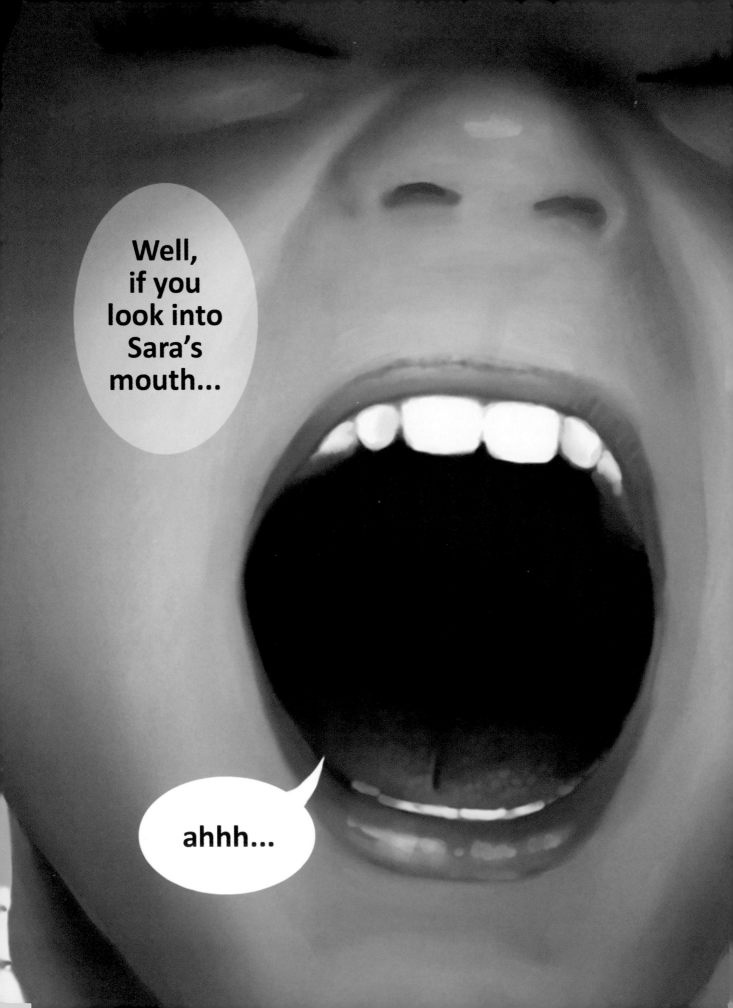

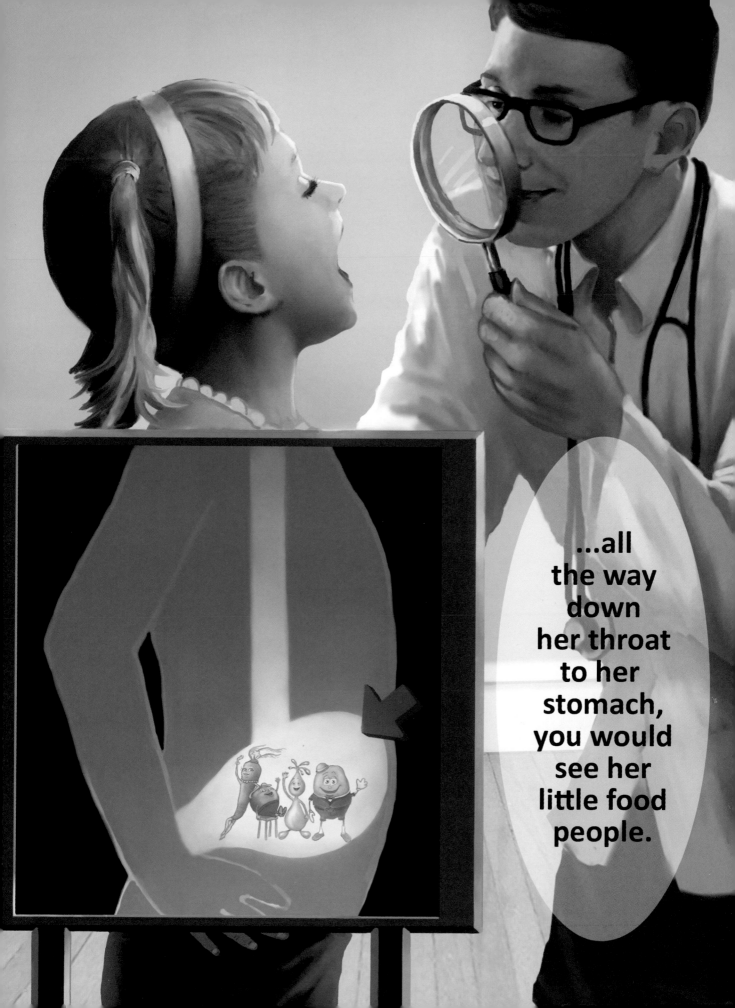

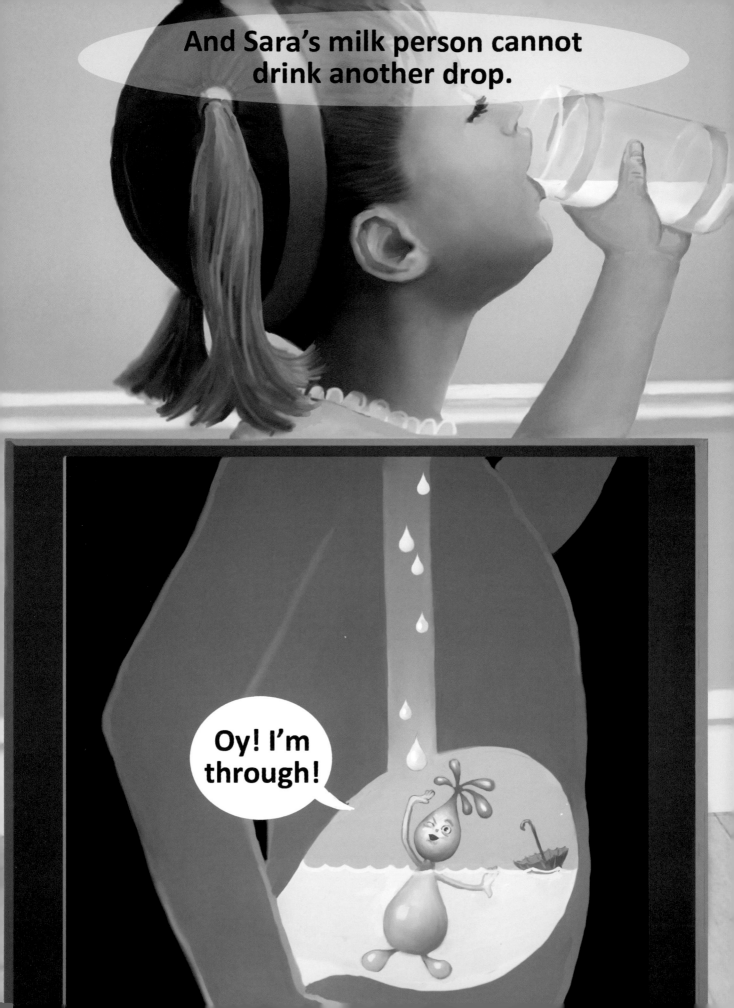

The End